W9-AAE-609

WITHDRAWN

OCT 1 6

Spellbound

An Imprint of Magic Wagon
abdopublishing.com

*Mom and Dad, If you ever doubted I'd become
a writer someday, I could never tell. —KRP*

*To Mom, the former cartoonist: for always
encouraging my inner artist. —BP*

abdopublishing.com

Published by Magic Wagon, a division of ABDO, PO Box
398166, Minneapolis, Minnesota 55439. Copyright © 2017 by
Abdo Consulting Group, Inc. International copyrights reserved
in all countries. No part of this book may be reproduced in
any form without written permission from the publisher.
Spellbound™ is a trademark and logo of Magic Wagon.

Printed in the United States of America, North Mankato,
Minnesota.
052016
092016

 **THIS BOOK CONTAINS
RECYCLED MATERIALS**

Written by Kelly Rogers
Illustrated by Betsy Peterschmidt
Edited by Heidi M.D. Elston and Megan M. Gunderson
Designed by Candice Keimig

Library of Congress Cataloging-in-Publication Data

Names: Rogers, Kelly, 1981- author. | Peterschmidt, Betsy, illustrator.

Title: The key / by Kelly Rogers ; illustrated by Betsy Peterschmidt.

Description: Minneapolis, MN : Magic Wagon, [2017] | Series: Rm. 201 |
    Summary: On her first day of seventh grade MJ meets the nice new science
    teacher--but when Ms. Fleek finally gets the door to the laboratory, room 201,
    open she changes and suddenly MJ does not want to go anywhere near
    her or that room.

Identifiers: LCCN 2016002436 (print) | LCCN 2016005467 (ebook) | ISBN
    9781624021695 (lib. bdg.) | ISBN 9781680790481 (ebook)

Subjects: LCSH: Horror tales. | Science teachers--Juvenile fiction. |
    Laboratories--Juvenile fiction. | Middle schools--Juvenile fiction. |
    CYAC: Horror stories. | Teachers--Fiction. | Laboratories--Fiction. |
    Middle schools--Fiction. | Schools--Fiction. | GSAFD: Horror fiction.

Classification: LCC PZ7.1.R65 Ke 2016 (print) | LCC PZ7.1.R65 (ebook) | DDC
    813.6--dc23

LC record available at http://lccn.loc.gov/2016002436

TABLE OF CONTENTS

CHAPTER 1
First Day Jitters

I was really nervous on my first day of seventh grade. But no way was I as nervous as my science teacher. I think we were Ms. Fleek's first ever science class.

Ms. Fleet

All last **summer**, I rode my bike to my new school a lot. My brother teased me. But I still went every week, just to get to know my way around. I **NEEDED** that.

So did Ms. Fleek, I guess. She was there every time. As weeks passed, Ms. Fleek FILLED her empty room. Posters and pictures. Colorful trays for homework. Bright folders for missing work.

But on the first day of school, Ms. Fleek herself was kind of a MESS. Dark circles under her eyes. Shirt tucked in halfway.

"Good morning, everyone," she said with a big smile. "Welcome to science class!" Her eyes *darted* around the room. No one spoke.

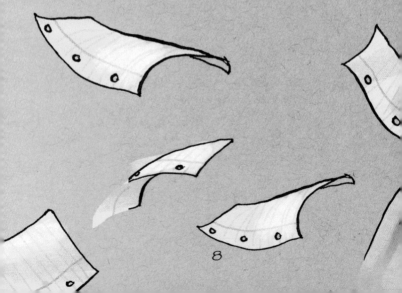

8

"My name is Emily. I, I mean, Ms. Fleek." Her face got very PINK. Some of the kids giggled. Not me. I know how it feels to be so **nervous**.

By the end of the first week, Ms. Fleek *seemed* to get into a groove.

Our first unit was on lab safety. We learned about goggles and GLOVES and what to do if there's an EMERGENCY. We even took a quiz. I got every question right!

12

Finally, it was time for our first lab. But when I got to RM. 201 the lab tables were empty.

"It has to be one of these!" Ms. Fleek mumbled. She had a huge ring of keys in her hand. She was trying to unlock a door at the front of her room. Her hands were SHAKING as she tried each key.

"Ms. Fleek?" I asked.

Ms. Fleek **JUMPED**!

"Oh, hi!" she said. She put a

smile on her face right away.

"It's MJ, right?"

I nodded. "Can I *help* you?"

Ms. Fleek turned back to the door. She tried the next key.

"I can't **OPEN** this door!" she said. "Our custodian says all the keys in the school are on this ring. But *none* of them are working. Looks like no lab today."

I wished Ms. Fleek **good luck** and turned to leave. As I turned, I thought I saw a *GLOW* under the door. Like someone had left a green LIGHT on inside the room.

We did a textbook assignment
that day. Ms. Fleek never did find
the right key.

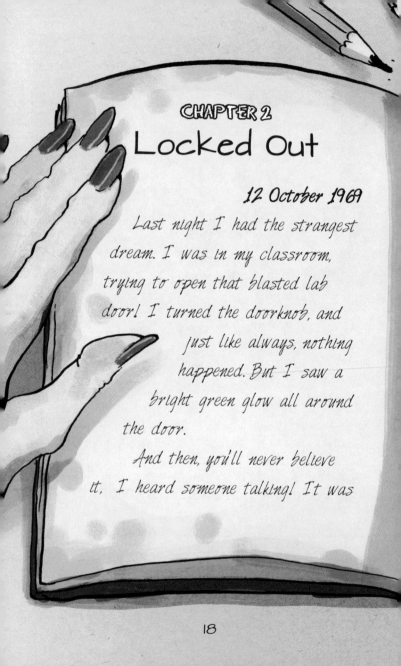

CHAPTER 2
Locked Out

12 October 1969

Last night I had the strangest dream. I was in my classroom, trying to open that blasted lab door! I turned the doorknob, and just like always, nothing happened. But I saw a bright green glow all around the door.

And then, you'll never believe it, I heard someone talking! It was

a deep voice. It sounded like it was saying, "Find a way, Emily. Find a way."

I woke up scared and sweating! I keep having these bad dreams. I love my job, but some days I feel almost too tired to teach.

– Emily Fleek

Ms. Fleek was not looking good. The circles under her eyes were getting darker. She looked SKINNIER, too.

She was still **looking** for the `right key` for that door. We mostly read our textbook, did worksheets, or took notes. Everyone was BORED.

Every time she passed that door, Ms. Fleek touched her head. Once, I saw her cover her mouth, like she felt sick. I kept thinking about that green LIGHT I'd seen.

One morning, I got to school early. I headed to RM. 201 but STOPPED at the door. Ms. Fleek was there with Ms. Hardwick, my English teacher.

23

"Are you *sure* you've tried every key?" asked Ms. Hardwick.

"I'm sure, Christine," **SNAPPED** Ms. Fleek.

Ms. Hardwick **FLINCHED**.

"I'm sorry, Christine. It's been a hard start to the year. I just wish I could *unlock* that door!"

Ms. Fleek breathed in deeply. "I thought I would be a good teacher! Make kids want to learn science!"

There was a long **PAUSE**.

"I can't even run a lab with them."

Then I heard quiet

crying. I walked away

quietly. Ms. Fleek

didn't need to know

I had heard.

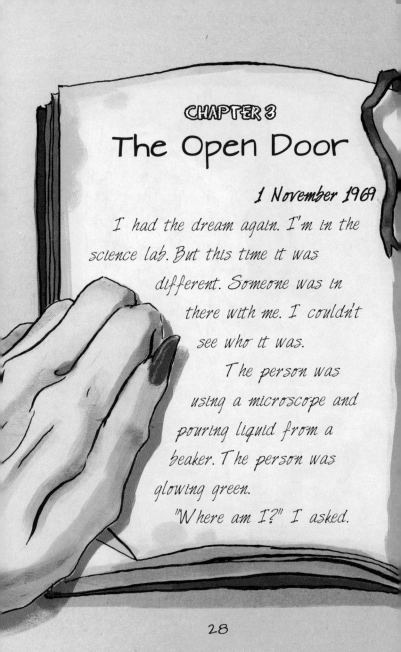

CHAPTER 3
The Open Door

1 November 1969

I had the dream again. I'm in the science lab. But this time it was different. Someone was in there with me. I couldn't see who it was.

The person was using a microscope and pouring liquid from a beaker. The person was glowing green.

"Where am I?" I asked.

"Right where you should be, Emily," the figure said back. "You finally found your way."

I started to go toward the figure. I could feel my heart beating, even in my dream. Then I woke up.

I am writing this down as soon as I woke up. Otherwise I might not believe it. No one would.

When I woke up from the dream, I had a key in my hand.

— Emily Fleek

"Ms. Fleek!" I said. I was the **FIRST** person in the room, as usual.

"You OPENED the door!"
For the first time, there were
microscopes on every table.

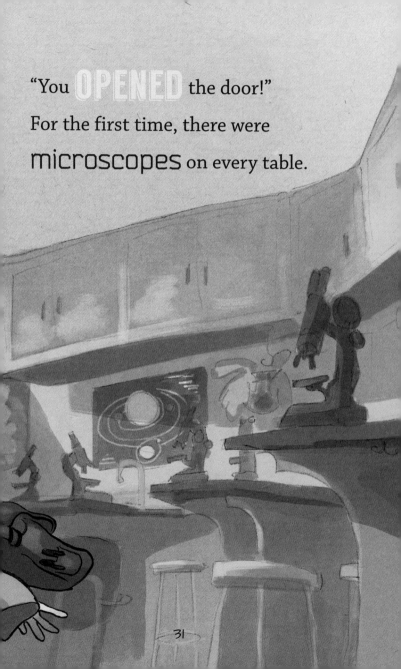

I noticed **changes** with Ms. Fleek right away, too. No dark circles. Shirt smooth and tucked in. And a single key hung on a **chain** around her neck.

"I found *my way*, MJ," Ms. Fleek said. Her mouth smiled, but it wasn't the same smile she had **yesterday**.

CHAPTER 4

Strange Changes

We've been able to do all of our science labs since Ms. Fleek opened **THAT DOOR** three months ago.

I was so excited when we first had the equipment out! But science class and Ms. Fleek have become strange. She doesn't smile as much. Well, not real smiles anyway.

In February, my Girl Scout troop brought **treats** to the teachers. I wheeled cookies and hot chocolate into the TEACHERS' LOUNGE.

"MJ!" Ms. Hardwick came up to me. "How are your classes?" she asked as she chose a cookie. "How is science?"

I paused.

"Science is FINE," I said, offering a cookie to the music teacher.

"But, MJ, how is **MS. FLEEK**?" Ms. Hardwick **pushed**.

"Um," I started.

Ms. Hardwick beat me again. Her face was level with mine. "Has she been acting strange in cla . . .?"

Ms. Hardwick looked over my head. Her eyes grew WIDE. She stood up STRAIGHT.

Ms. Fleek was standing in the DOORWAY.

I had never noticed before how green her *eyes* were. They **BURNED** into Ms. Hardwick.

"Christine?" Ms. Fleek asked with that *weird* smile. "Did you get your cookie?"

Ms. Hardwick looked like a **scared** rabbit. She didn't say anything.

She **dropped** her cookie and left the room.

Ms. Fleek SNATCHED a cookie from my tray. Her eyes sparkled. "See you in class, MJ."

I LEFT the lounge without my tray.

Spring break was a month later. Ms. Hardwick *NEVER CAME BACK* after break.

I began to make math class my first stop in the morning. I didn't go to RM. 201 unless I had to.

We kept using the lab equipment. But any time that door **OPENED**, I held my head. I *covered* my mouth. I felt **sick**.

DO NOT ENTER

STAFF ONLY

NO ENTRY

That summer after seventh grade, I rode my bike to the **BEACH**. I rode my bike to the *mall*. I **NEVER** went to the school.

And when I had to go back in the fall, I stayed **AWAY** from RM. 201.